Colton

Helping Santa

My First Christmas Adventure with Grandma

Illustrated by

Bert Dodson

www.bunkerhillpublishing.com
by Bunker Hill Publishing Inc.
285 River Road, Piermont
New Hampshire 03779, USA

10 9 8 7 6 5 4 3 2 1

Library of Congress Control Number: 2011925664
ISBN 978-1-59373-093-2

Designed by Joe Lops
Printed in China by Jade Productions

Dear Readers,

After much searching, we have been unable to locate the original author of this story. However, not knowing who first told this tale does not lessen its message, which fully encompasses the spirit of Christmas and reassures us that we never have to stop believing in Santa Claus. In fact, we believe that we can carry Santa with us always—and that *each of us* can be his helper when we see someone in need.

In the spirit of this belief, we have chosen to contribute to **One Warm Coat**, a nationwide organization whose mission is to make sure that everyone who needs a warm coat can get one in his or her hometown, easily, free of charge. We will give a percentage of the money earned from the sale of this book to **One Warm Coat** to support its work. Learn about its activities and where you can donate a coat at www.onewarmcoat.org.

Once you've read this endearing story, we know you will join us in helping Santa this year and for many years to come.

Happy Holidays!
Carole and Ib Bellew
And all of us at Bunker Hill Publishing

My first Christmas adventure with Grandma,
I remember tearing across town on my bike to visit
her the day my big sister dropped the bomb:
“There is no Santa Claus,” she jeered.
“Even dummies know that!”

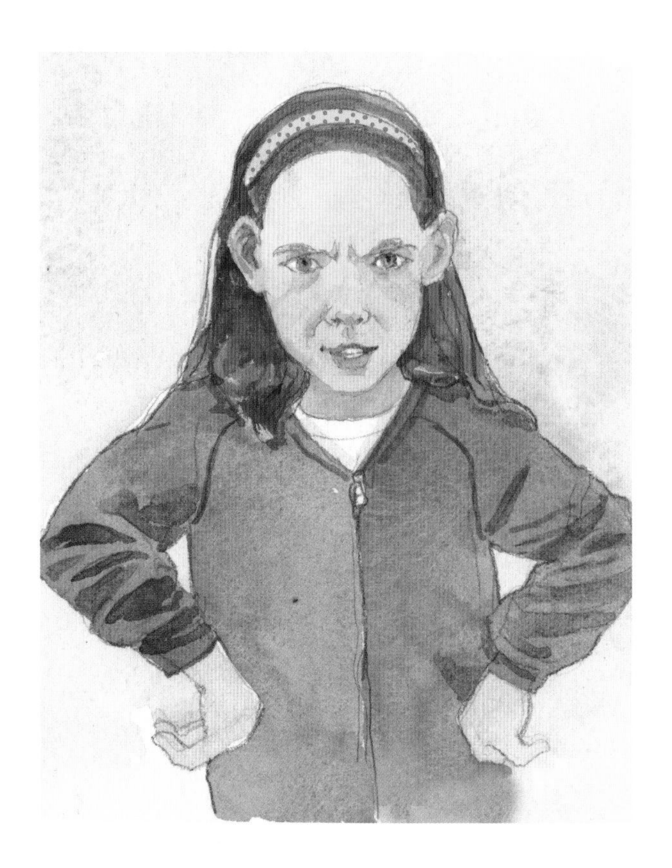

My grandma was not the gushy kind, never had been. I fled to her that day because I knew she would be straight with me. I knew Grandma always told the truth, and I knew that the truth always went down a whole lot easier when swallowed with one of her world-famous cinnamon buns. I knew they were world-famous because Grandma said so. And so it had to be true.

Grandma was home, and the buns were still warm. Between bites, I told her everything. She was ready for me. " No Santa Claus?" she snorted. "Ridiculous! Don't believe it. That rumor has been going around for years, and it makes me mad, just plain mad!"

“Now put on your coat, and let’s go.”
she said.
“Go? Go where, Grandma?” I asked.
I hadn’t even finished my second
world-famous cinnamon bun.

Where turned out to be Hill's 5 & 10 Variety store, the one shop in town that had a little bit of just about everything.

As we walked through its doors, Grandma handed me ten dollars. That was a bundle in those days. “Take this money,” she said, “and buy something for someone who needs it.

“I’ll wait for you in the car.” Then she turned and walked out of Hill’s.

I was only eight years old. I'd often gone shopping with my mother, but never had I bought anything all by myself.

The store seemed big and crowded, full of people scrambling to finish up their Christmas shopping.

For a few moments I just stood there, confused, clutching that ten dollar bill, wondering what to buy and who on earth to buy it for. I thought of everybody I knew: my family, my friends, my neighbors, the kids at school, and the people who went to my church.

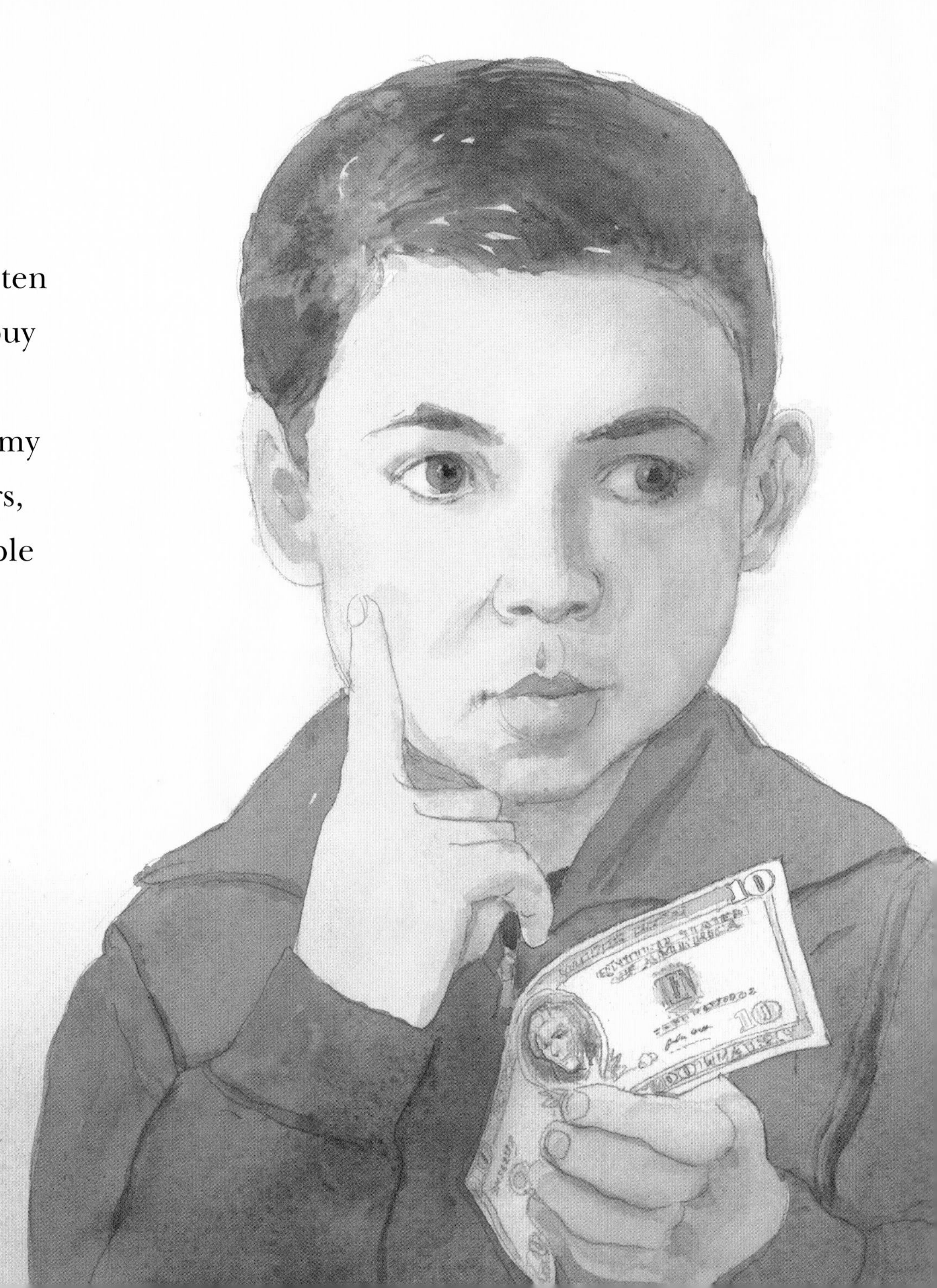

I was just about thought out when I suddenly remembered Bobby Decker. He was a kid with bad breath and messy hair, and he sat right behind me in Mrs. Pollock's grade-two class. Bobby Decker didn't have a coat. I knew that because he never went out to recess during the winter, not once.

His mother always wrote a note, telling the teacher that he had a cough, but all of us kids knew that Bobby Decker didn't have a cough; he just didn't have a good warm coat to wear outside.

I fingered the ten-dollar bill with growing excitement. I would buy Bobby Decker a coat!

I settled on a red corduroy one that had a hood on it. It looked real warm, just what he would need for playing outside.

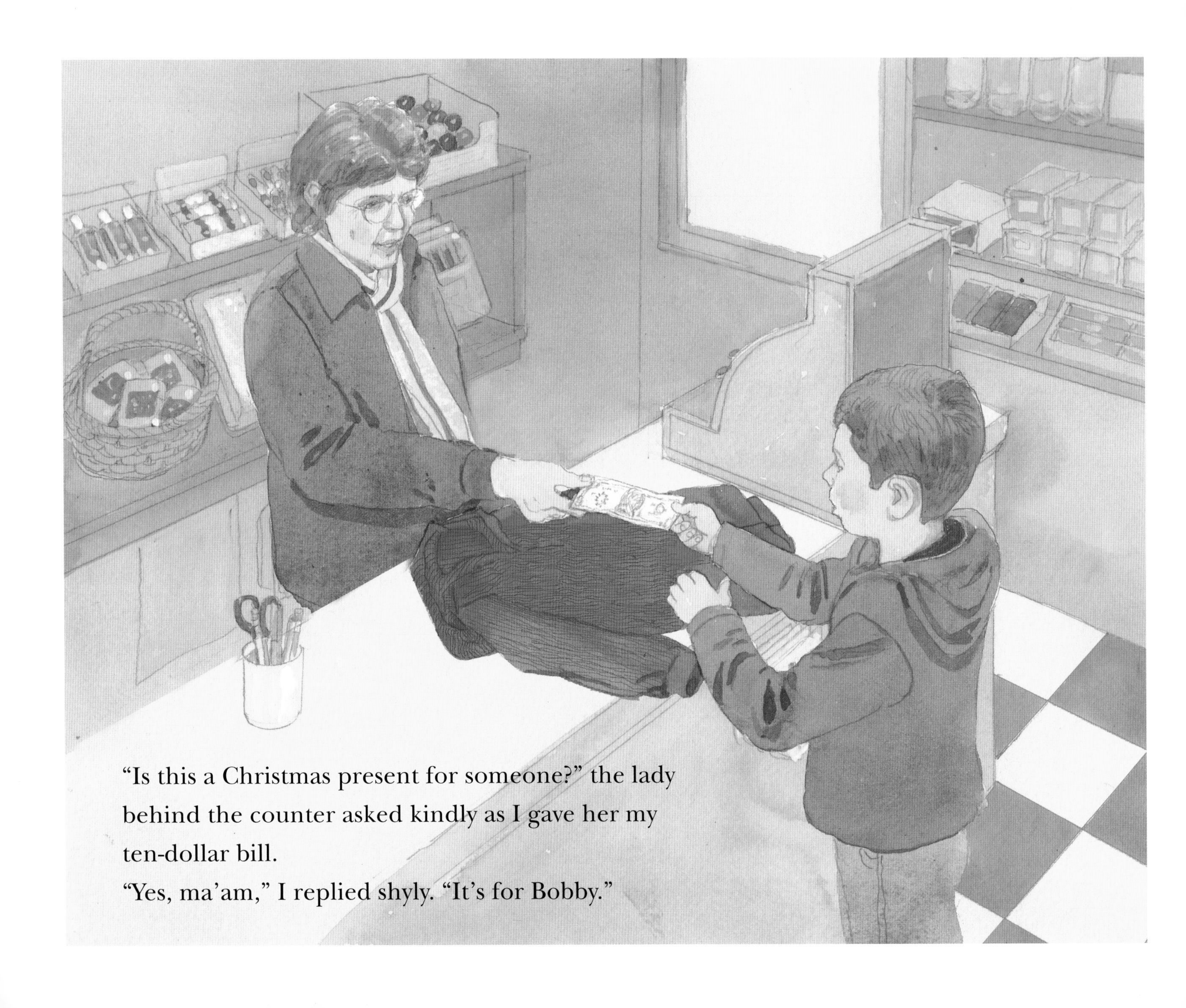

"Is this a Christmas present for someone?" the lady behind the counter asked kindly as I gave her my ten-dollar bill.

"Yes, ma'am," I replied shyly. "It's for Bobby."

The nice lady smiled at me as I told her about how Bobby really needed a good winter coat. I didn't get any change, but she put the coat in a bag, smiled again, and wished me a merry Christmas.

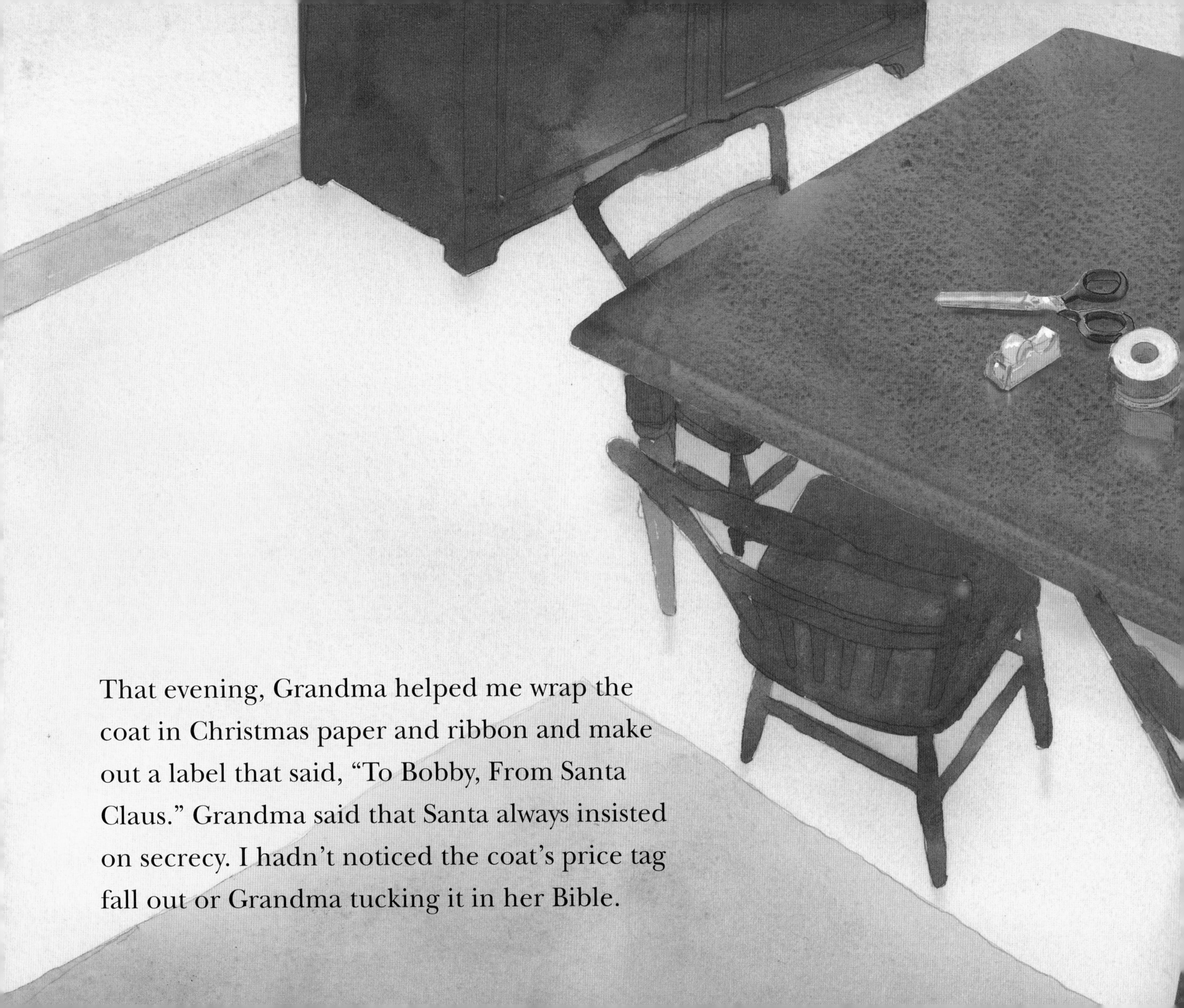

That evening, Grandma helped me wrap the coat in Christmas paper and ribbon and make out a label that said, "To Bobby, From Santa Claus." Grandma said that Santa always insisted on secrecy. I hadn't noticed the coat's price tag fall out or Grandma tucking it in her Bible.

to

Then she drove me over to Bobby Decker's house, explaining as we went that I was now and forever officially one of Santa's elves.

Grandma parked down the street from Bobby's house, and she and I crept up noiselessly and hid in the bushes by his front walk.

Then Grandma gave me a nudge. "All right, Santa's helper," she whispered, "get going."

I took a deep breath, dashed for his front porch, threw the present down, pounded his door and flew back to the safety of the bushes and Grandma.

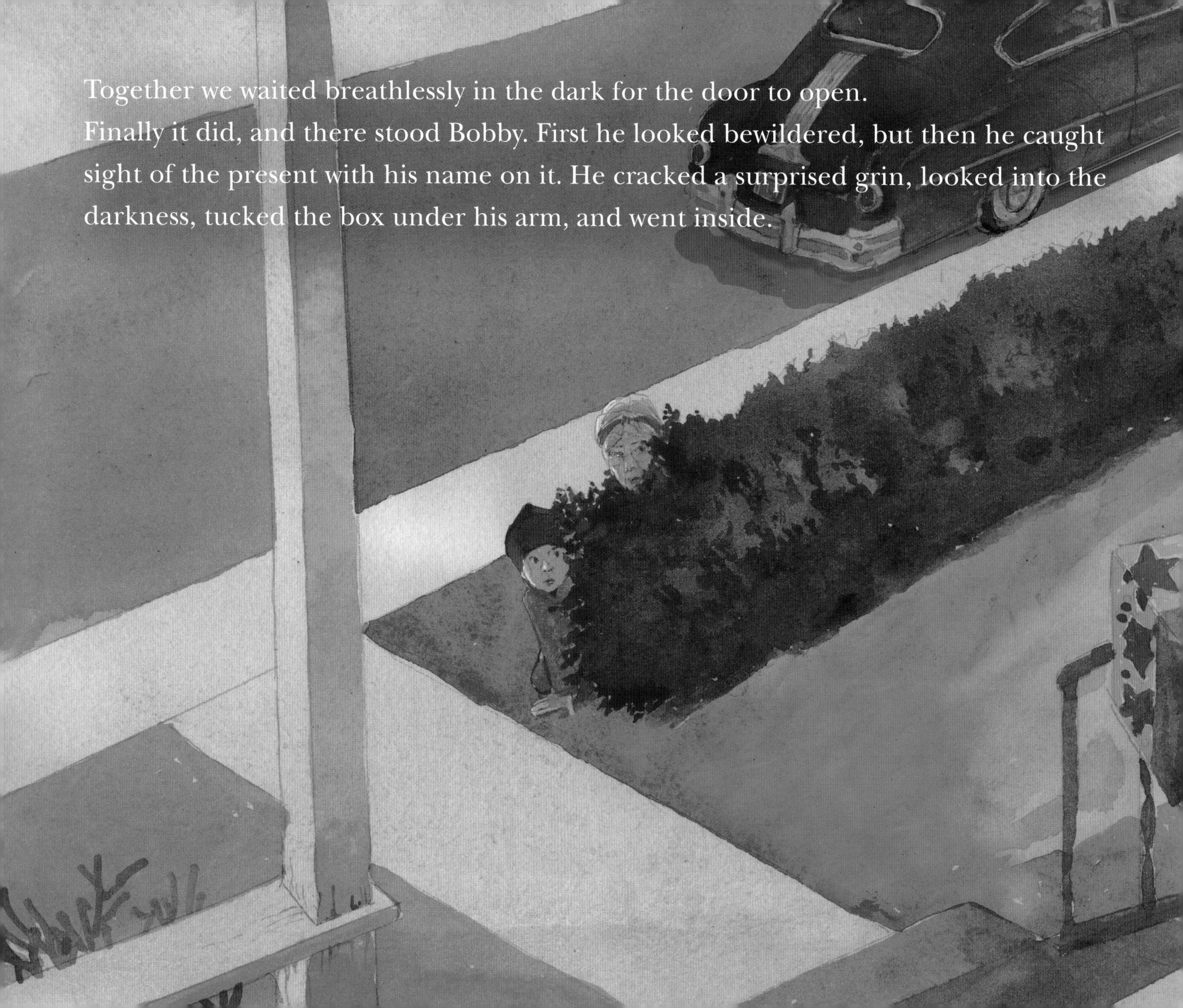

Together we waited breathlessly in the dark for the door to open.

Finally it did, and there stood Bobby. First he looked bewildered, but then he caught sight of the present with his name on it. He cracked a surprised grin, looked into the darkness, tucked the box under his arm, and went inside.

That night, I realized that those awful rumors about Santa Claus were just what Grandma said they were, *ridiculous*. Santa was alive and well, and we were on his team.

Fifty years haven't dimmed the thrill of those moments spent shivering, beside my grandma, in Bobby Decker's bushes. I still have Grandma's Bible, with the price tag tucked inside, $19.95. That winter Bobby wore his coat every day on the playground.

May we always believe in the magic of Santa Claus!